SEP   2019

Jayson TATUM

A ROBBIE READER

**Tammy
Gagne**

PUBLISHERS

2001 SW 31st Avenue
Hallandale, FL 33009

www.mitchelllane.com

First Edition, 2020.
Author: Tammy Gagne
Designer: Ed Morgan
Editor: Lisa Petrillo

Series: Robbie Reader
Title: Jayson Tatum / by Tammy Gagne

Hallandale, FL : Mitchell Lane Publishers, [2020]

Library bound ISBN: 9781680205183
eBook ISBN: 9781680205190

Contents

GETTING it Done, Together

"Mom, it's almost time for my game," Toby said. He was hoping to cut his multiplication practice short. But deep down he knew his mother wouldn't budge.

"Just a few more," she promised. "How about three times nine?"

"Twenty-seven," he answered proudly. She had been quizzing him every night this week, helping him prepare for his big test tomorrow. He appreciated her help. When he started, multiplication felt overwhelming. Now she had a hard time stumping him.

"Good job," she said as she reached for the television remote.

"Hey, no fair!" Toby scolded. She never allowed him to watch TV while studying. "If I can't watch, neither can you."

"I'm not watching," she replied while scrolling through the electronic guide. She set the recorder for the Boston Celtics game. "I'm just making sure I don't miss my second-favorite basketball player." She was talking about Jayson Tatum. Toby was her favorite.

He had forgotten that the Celtics were playing tonight. Toby loved that his mother enjoyed basketball as much as he did. His father liked it, too. But he lived on the West Coast now. Toby's mom was raising their son by herself. Still, she always made it to his games and made sure he stayed on top of his school work.

Toby had heard that Jayson Tatum was also raised by a single mother. Tatum was so inspired by her that he started a foundation to help other single moms. Maybe one day Toby would become a famous basketball player like his idol. He could picture his own mom cheering him on in the stands as he sank three-pointers.

"What are you smiling about?" his mother asked just then.

"Just how much I love you, Mom," he answered.

"I love you, too, kiddo. But that's not going to get you out of finishing your math," she said. "Now, what's eight times nine?"

FOLLOWING
Their *Dreams*

Jayson Tatum was born March 3, 1978, in St. Louis, Missouri. His mother, Brandy Cole, had long dreamed of becoming a lawyer. His father, Justin Tatum, was a student and basketball player at Saint Louis University. Determined to follow her dreams, Brandy enrolled in the University of Missouri-Saint Louis while raising Jayson.

Tatum drives the ball against Toronto Raptors forward Pascal Siakam in January 2019.

As a child, Jayson would visit his father in the college basketball team locker room. Then Justin received an opportunity to turn professional — on a basketball team in the Netherlands thousands of miles away. Brandy and Justin made the situation work so Jayson could have both parents involved in his life. She even took Jayson to visit his father in Europe as often as she could.

Life wasn't always easy. But Brandy taught Jayson that he too could do anything he set his mind to. He learned this lesson by watching his parents succeed. Sometimes Brandy took Jayson with her to classes at the university. If her parents could not watch him, she thought it was better to tote him along than for her to miss a class.

Jayson also learned that his dreams mattered after his first-grade teacher asked him what he wanted to be when he grew up. When the little boy told her he dreamed of playing in the National Basketball Association (NBA), he became upset when his teacher tried to offer other choices. His mother Brandy visited the teacher the next day, as she later told a reporter of the event: "I said, 'Ma'am, with all due respect, if you ask him a question and he answers, I don't think it's appropriate to tell him that's something he can't achieve when I'm at home telling him anything he can dream is possible.'" Fortunately, with his mother helping him believe in his dreams, it helped Jayson believe too.

Jayson always believed he could make it to the NBA, thanks to his mother.

WORKING *Hard*

Jayson did not **inherit** his mother's dream for him of becoming a lawyer. One day while she was studying property law, he told her he never wanted to study topics that he found boring. He did inherit his father's love for basketball, though. Jayson again shared his dream of becoming a professional athlete with his mother. She told him that he would have to work hard to achieve that goal.

Jayson was one of the hardest-working players on the basketball court at Chaminade College Prepatory.

Soon Jayson was getting up early every morning and heading to the gym before school. He would practice for an hour and a half before his classes began. His hard work did not go unnoticed. His high school coach, Frank Bennett, noticed that Jayson showed up every morning even before he did.

After his father Justin's professional career ended, he returned home to coach basketball at Christian Brothers College High School in Missouri. Jayson wanted to play for his father. But he was already a student at a private high school called Chaminade College Preparatory. If he switched schools he would have had to miss a year of playing basketball for his new school because of laws restricting high school **transfers** for sports. So Jayson stayed with his school and played against the team his father coached. And like everything else, he gave it his all. His team lost.

After losing that first game against Christian Brothers, Jayson was determined not to let it happen again. He went on to play seven more games against his father's team as a member of the Chaminade Red Devils. And he won every single one. In a single game during his senior year, Jayson scored 46 points against Christian Brothers before the end of the third quarter. When a **defender** grabbed him to keep him from scoring,

Jayson made the jump shot with the other player hanging off his shoulder. Coach Bennett told a reporter from ESPN, "It was one of those moments when we realized, 'He really can't be stopped.'"

None of Jayson's high school opponents could match his focus for the game.

BECOMING a *Blue Devil*

As the star of Chaminade College Prep basketball team, Jayson received a lot of attention from college **recruiters**. Schools in numerous states wanted Jayson Tatum to play for them. After a visit to Durham, North Carolina, he committed to attend Duke University for the fall of 2016. He was turning from a Red Devil into a Blue Devil. He liked Duke's **academic** program. And he felt an instant bond with the basketball staff. In an interview with a reporter from ESPN, Tatum said, "My relationships with the Duke coaches were the best, and they made me a priority. They did the best job of recruiting me and have been at almost all my games, and that means a lot."

Many freshmen basketball players start their college careers on the bench. They learn from watching their older teammates on the court. They then get their chance to contribute to the team. But Tatum started playing in Duke games immediately. And right away, he stood out even among the more experienced players. It didn't hurt that he had grown to a height of 6-feet, 8-inches. But his advantage was clearly his ability.

Tatum's passion for the sport remained high as he moved on to college ball in 2016.

As a **forward** for the Duke Blue Devils, Tatum was averaging 16.9 points and 7.3 rebounds per game. His coaches were confident that he could help lead the team to the playoffs in the 2016–2017 season. They also saw the season as his one chance to do so. They knew that a player with his talent would likely enter the NBA draft following his first year of college ball.

The Blue Devils players enjoyed their share of victories with Tatum on their side. The team won the Atlantic Coast Conference (ACC) Championship. But they were eliminated from the National Collegiate Athletic Association (NCAA) Tournament when North Carolina beat them in the second round. Tatum's college career was ending. But his professional career was just around the corner.

Tatum dunks the ball during the first half
against the Troy Trojans in the first round of
the 2017 NCAA Tournament.

Doing HIS PART as a *Pro*

When Tatum entered the NBA draft in June 2017, the move was far from a long shot. Many people expected him to be among the first players chosen, and they were right. The Boston Celtics selected Tatum as the No. 3 pick of the first round. The Celtics officials saw him as one of the most versatile players they could have chosen. At Duke he had shown that he excelled playing either forward position. He was also skilled at defending.

Tatum joined his new professional team with ease. As soon as his rookie season began, he knew exactly where he needed to be on the court. He wasn't just playing the same way he did in high school and college, where he was the standout athlete. Now, he was working with many other players who were just as talented as he was. They were succeeding at getting the ball to him. And he was **dependably** scoring with it. The team finished the season just one game away from the NBA Finals.

Tatum drives to the basket past Brooklyn Nets forward DeMarre Carroll in December 2017.

During the regular season, Tatum averaged 13.9 points per game. He fared even better in the post-season, upping his average to 18.2 points. Tatum finished his first post-season with 351 points, just one shy of the rookie record created by legendary player Kareem Abdul-Jabbar. The young player from St. Louis had made his dream of playing professional basketball a reality. And now he was making a name for himself as a valuable team player.

Showing his great jumping ability, Tatum dunks the ball during a game against the Brooklyn Nets in January 2019.

THERE IS NO

Tatum with his mom Brandy Cole. He lends his time to
many charities and started his own organization to
help children, especially families with single mothers
because he was raised by one.

Tatum has also made a name for himself off the court with the Jayson Tatum Foundation. He created the charity organization that joined with a shelter to help single mothers and their kids. Through the charity, he hopes to help struggling single moms with expenses such as for heating, electricity, and childcare.

"I was fortunate enough to make it to where I want to be," Tatum told a reporter from CBS Sports. "There could be other kids as talented or more talented than me in whatever they want to be." He wants to make sure they get the chance to pursue their dreams—just like he did.

Timeline

1998   Born on March 3

2012   Starts playing on the Chaminade Red Devils as a high school freshman

2016   Begins freshman year at Duke University, playing for the Blue Devils

2017   Wins the ACC Championship with his Duke Blue Devils team

         Picked as No. 3 draft pick by Boston Celtics

2018   Finishes rookie season one point shy of Kareem Abdul-Jabbar's post-season rookie record

Find Out More

Boston Celtics
https://www.nba.com/celtics/

ESPN, Jayson Tatum
http://www.espn.com/nba/player/_/id/4065648/jayson-tatum

Moussavi, Sam and Kissock, Heather. *Boston Celtics*. New York: AV2 by Weigl, 2016.
NBA website, Jayson Tatum.

http://www.nba.com/players/jayson/tatum/1628369
Whiting, Jim. *Boston Celtics*. Mankato, MN: Creative Education, 2018.

Works Consulted

"Celtics take scorer Jayson Tatum with No. 3 pick in draft." *USA Today*, June 22, 2017.
https://www.usatoday.com/story/sports/nba/2017/06/22/celtics-select-jayson-tatum-with-no-3-pick-in-draft/103122924/

"Duke Basketball: Why the 2016-2017 Season Was Really a Success." ACCSports.com, May 26, 2017.
https://accsports.com/acc-news/basketball/duke-basketball-season-success/

Biancardi, Paul. "Jayson Tatum commits to Duke." ESPN, July 12, 2015.
http://www.espn.com/college-sports/recruiting/basketball/mens/story/_/id/13244364/jayson-tatum-no-2-recruit-espn-class-2016-commits-duke-blue-devils

Forgrave, Reid. "'Built for Basketball': Jayson Tatum Was Born and Raised to Be an NBA Star." *Bleacher Report*, June 19, 2017.
https://bleacherreport.com/articles/2711366-built-for-basketball-jayson-tatum-was-born-and-raised-to-be-an-nba-star

Forgrave, Reid. "How Celtics' Jayson Tatum is using his NBA success to power a foundation for single mothers like his own." *CBS Sports*, November 21, 2018.
https://www.cbssports.com/nba/news/how-celtics-jayson-tatum-is-using-his-nba-success-to-power-a-foundation-for-single-mothers-like-his-own/

Works Consulted *continued*

Goodman, Jeff. "Tatum's relationship with his mother led him to Duke." ESPN, November 9, 2016.
http://www.espn.com/mens-college-basketball/story/_/id/17969404/duke-blue-devils-jayson-tatum-relationship-mother

MacMulan, Jackie. "Thrust into the spotlight, Boston's Jayson Tatum is ready for prime time." ESPN, October 16, 2018.
http://www.espn.com/nba/story/_/id/24989322/thrust-spotlight-boston-jayson-tatum-ready-prime

Smith, Jeff. "Jayson Tatum falls one point shy of tying amazing NBA playoff record." *Celts* Wire, May 27, 2018.
https://celticswire.usatoday.com/2018/05/27/jayson-tatum-celtics-nba-playoff-record-kareem-abdul-jabbar-news-stats/

Tjarks, Jonathan. "What Jayson Tatum's Success Tells Us About the Future of NBA Drafting." *The Ringer*, November 30, 2016.
https://www.theringer.com/nba/2017/11/30/16717774/jayson-tatum-boston-celtics-nba-draft-wings

Zagoria, Adam. "Jayson Tatum Is the Breakout Star of Duke's Freshman Class." *The New York Times*, March 17, 2017.
https://www.nytimes.com/2017/03/17/sports/ncaabasketball/tatum-is-the-breakout-star-of-dukes-freshman-class.html

Glossary

academic
Relating to school and studying

defender
A player who tries to keep the opposite team from scoring

dependably
Done with consistency that others can count on

forward
A basketball position that tries to score against the opposite team

inherit
To receive a trait from a parent or other relative

recruiter
A person whose job it is to find a person with certain talents

transfer
To move from one school to another

Index

About the Author

Tammy Gagne has written more than 200 books for both adults and children. As a lifelong New Englander, she remains loyal to the Boston Celtics—the team that helped Jayson Tatum's dreams come true. Her work has led her to count Jayson along with several other athletes to become her favorites. She has also profiled the great life stories for Mitchell Lane of sports stars Todd Gurley and Deshaun Watson.